Ciara

A Cinderella Story

Ciara

A Cinderella Story

Written by Angela Hazelray

Illustrated by Tiyah Crockett

KEEN VISION PUBLISHING

Limits of Liability and Disclaimer of Warranty
The author and publisher shall not be liable for your misuse of this material. This book is strictly for informational purposes. The purpose of this book is to educate and entertain. The author and publisher do not guarantee anyone following these techniques, suggestions, tips, ideas, or strategies will become successful. The author and publisher shall have neither liability nor responsibility to anyone with respect to any loss or damage caused, or alleged to be caused, directly or indirectly by the information contained in this book. Views expressed in this publication do not necessarily reflect the views of the publisher.

Printed in the United States of America
Keen Vision Publishing, LLC
www.publishwithKVP.com
ISBN: 978-1-948270-96-0

For my mom who always taught me to know my worth.

"You are fearfully and wonderfully made."
Psalm 139:14

Hello! My name is Ciara. I am the girl who walked away from the prince on our wedding day.

I know what you're *thinking*...
but let me tell you my side of the story.....

Long ago, I lived with my mom and dad. They always told me to remember three things, *"Stay true to yourself. Know your worth. Never settle."*

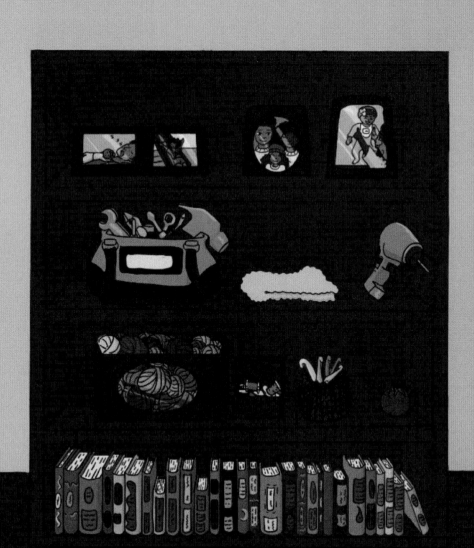

One day, my mother became ill. There was nothing the doctors could do to help her get better. After my mother's death, life became dark and lonely. My dad and I had each other, *but nothing was the same.*

To make me happy, my dad decided to get married. I was excited to have a mother and was delighted to find out that she had two daughters as well. Unfortunately, when my dad left for work, they treated me horribly. I was their servant until my father came home. I didn't tell my dad because he seemed so happy with his new wife.

One day there was a knock at our door. When my stepmother opened the door, there was a man wearing beautiful clothes adorned with jewels. I listened to their conversation from the stairs.

"Greetings!" he addressed her.

"What can I do for you?" my stepmother answered.

"I have come to invite your daughters to the royal ball." he replied.

"Will the prince be there?" she inquired.

"Yes. How many invites should I leave?" the man asked.

"I have two daughters." my stepmother replied.

"I see three young ladies."

"She is not going."

"Every young lady must attend the ball per the Prince's request. You surely wouldn't want to dismiss the King's orders, would you?" the man said.

"He wouldn't want me to bring her wearing rags would he?"

"Surely you'll find her something more appropriate."

The messenger turned and walked away. Elated, I danced about the room.

My stepmother closed the door. "Sit down. You're not going anywhere."

"But he said everyone must go."

"You have nothing to wear and you will not embarrass me. Trust me. No one will notice that you aren't there."

The next day, my sisters headed to the shops to find gowns for the ball. I was overwhelmed with sadness, but I didn't want to show it.

"We thought about having you make them, but decided you could never make a dress beautiful enough for the ball," the sisters laughed.

I held every tear for as long as I could. As soon as they left I ran to the pond behind our house. I watched as my tears dropped into the pond.

Suddenly, I saw a familiar face.

"Mama?" I cried.

"Yes." she responded.

I could not believe my eyes.

"Oh, mama! I have missed you. Dad has married a witch with two witch children."

"I know, Ciara. I also know how you let them treat you. Do you remember what your dad and I always told you?"

"Yes ma'am. *Stay true to yourself. Know your worth. Never settle.*"

"One last thing," mom said, "Go to the ball."

On the day of the ball, I waited until my stepmom and sisters were gone before I got ready. I combed my hair up in a bun and slipped into my gown that I worked on while they slept. I headed downstairs and was greeted by my father.

"You look stunning."

"Thank you. I'm headed to the ball," I replied.

Dad looked me over and landed at my worn shoes. While I was great at sewing, I was not a shoemaker.

"I have something for you. I kept a pair of your mom's shoes."

Dad ran into his room and came back with the most beautiful shoes. I quickly put them on and hurried out the door.

The ball was all I had imagined. I was impressed until I saw the prince. I watched as he moved throughout the crowd and danced with every girl. Before he took their hand, he examined them from head to toe. If he didn't like what he saw, he walked to the next girl.

Finally, he made his way to me. It was as if the room stopped and we were the only two at the ball. He was charming, so I accepted his invitation to dance. He knew how to make a girl smile. As I gazed around the room, everyone's eyes were watching us.

As I watched the crowd, I spotted my step-witches leaving the ball. I quickly snapped back to reality.

"I'm sorry," I told the prince. "I have to leave."

I ran so fast, I didn't realize I'd lost a shoe.

The next day, I overheard my step sisters talking about the ball.

"The prince was such a charmer," one sister said.

"Yes, I loved the way we danced together," the other joined in.

"Oh! Me too, he is a great dancer."

"When we danced he looked right into my eyes."

"Well, when we danced he held me tightly in his arms."

"He did that with everyone."

The girls glared at one another like bulls in battle. I chuckled silently to myself.

"No need to argue," my stepmother interjected. "Both of you have a chance with the prince. He seemed to like all the young ladies equally. Except for that one girl. He talked and danced with her longer than any other girl in the room."

A familiar knock pounded on the door.

"Good evening, ladies. The prince is seeking the lady who owns this shoe." the messenger announced.

Both of my stepsisters tried on the shoe. I watched as they squeezed, stretched, and strained my mama's shoe until the messenger nearly had to pry it out of their hands.

"How about you? You are the last lady today. So many ladies have tried to fit this shoe."

"How many?" I questioned.

"Too many to keep track of," the messenger responded.

"You mean everyone has had their foot in my shoe?" I questioned.

"What do you mean your shoe?" asked the messenger.

I wasn't sure how to respond. The messenger slid the slipper on my foot. Before the step witches could say anything, the messenger carried me away to prepare for the prince.

When I met with the prince all he did was compliment himself.

"I am the next king. I am the richest man in the land. Don't you feel lucky to marry a man like me?" the prince asked.

He never asked me anything about me. I grew tired of hearing him go on and on about himself. So, I told him how I liked to sew.

"No need, my dear. You won't need that here."

I loved the castle, the garments, and being waited on for a change, however I had dreams too. I wanted to tell him but I was afraid he would refuse to marry me.

The day of our wedding finally arrived. I should have been happy and feeling like the most beautiful girl in the world, but I was sad. Every time I looked in the mirror the face looking back at me was concerned. I put on my wedding dress to wash away my worries, but I was only reminded that it was a dress prepared for me. I had always dreamed of making my own dress for my wedding. My dress reminded me that marrying the prince meant leaving behind all of my dreams.

"Ciara, it's time," called the messenger.

I walked down the aisle of my wedding full of people I didn't know. My step witches were there but they didn't count. Luckily, I had my dad next to me.

The Prince looked perfect, not a hair out of place. For a moment, I could just get over all the things he didn't know about me. Maybe one day he would want to know me. Maybe one day we would be friends and do fun things and travel places. Maybe one day we…

"Ciara,"

I quickly popped back to reality.

"Do you take this man to be your husband?"

I didn't know what to say. I burst into tears in front of everyone. I could hear the moans of the disgruntled guests.

The prince leaned over to whisper what I thought would be comforting words. "This is embarrassing. Stop that crying and answer the question."

My dad gave me his handkerchief. As I wiped my eyes, I noticed the answer to my dilemma engraved beautifully in the cloth.

Shocking the crowd, I ran away.

Later, the messenger found me to let me know that the Prince was shocked, yet proud of my decision. "He wanted you to have your crown." I was declared a Forever Princess. I am now the designer of everything royal.

And I lived happily ever after.

Connect with the Author

Thank you for reading, *Ciara: A Cinderella Story.* Angela looks forward to connecting with you. Here are a few ways you can connect with the author and stay updated on new releases, speaking engagements, products, and more.

FACEBOOK   ANGELA HAZELRAY
INSTAGRAM   @angeladavisauthor
WEBSITE   sites.google.com/view/angelahazelray/home

Made in the USA
Columbia, SC
30 April 2021